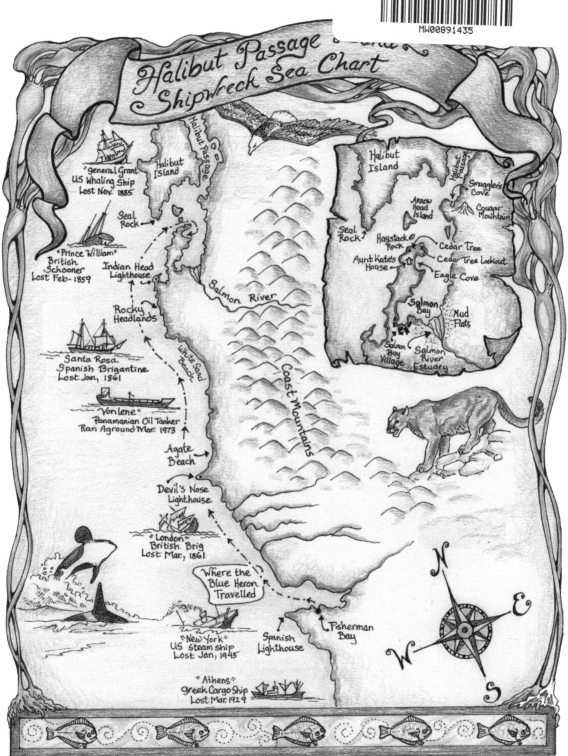

Halibut Passage Island
Shipwreck Sea Chart

"General Grant"
US Whaling
Ship
Lost Nov. 1885

Halibut
Island

Halibut Passage

Seal
Rock

"Prince William"
British
Schooner
Lost Feb. 1859

Indian Head
Lighthouse

Rocky
Headlands

Salmon River

Santa Rosa
Spanish Brigantine
Lost Jan. 1861

White Sand Beach

"Von lene"
Panamanian Oil Tanker
Ran Aground Mar. 1973

Coast Mountains

Agate
Beach

Devil's Nose
Lighthouse

"London"
British Brig
Lost Mar. 1861

Where the
Blue Heron
Travelled

"New York"
US steam ship
Lost Jan. 1945

Spanish
Lighthouse

Fisherman Bay

"Athens"
Greek Cargo Ship
Lost Mar. 1929

Halibut
Island

Halibut Passage

Smuggler's
Cove

Arrow
Head
Island

Cougar
Mountain

Seal
Rock

Haystack
Rock

Cedar Tree

Aunt Kate's
House

Cedar Tree Lookout

Eagle Cove

Salmon
Bay

Mud
Flats

Salmon
Bay
Village

Salmon
River
Estuary

N
E
W
S

# EXPLORE the WILD COAST

## with SAM and CRYSTAL

Gloria Snively    ILLUSTRATED BY Karen Gillmore

HERITAGE

VICTORIA · VANCOUVER · CALGARY

To my husband, John Corsiglia, for his wisdom and constant kindness; my daughter, Alicia; my grandchildren, Eulalie and Gryphon; and all children, whose love of nature has served as a source of inspiration. May the planet remain beautiful and rich with its great diversity of species for all generations to come.

Heritage House Publishing Company Ltd.
heritagehouse.ca

CATALOGUING INFORMATION AVAILABLE FROM
LIBRARY AND ARCHIVES CANADA

978-1-77203-167-6 (cloth)
978-1-77203-253-6 (pbk)
978-1-77203-169-0 (epdf)

Edited by Lara Kordic
Cover and interior illustrations by Karen Gillmore
Cover and interior book design by Jacqui Thomas

The interior of this book was produced on FSC®-certified, acid-free paper, processed chlorine free, and printed with vegetable-based inks.

We acknowledge the financial support of the Government of Canada through the Canada Book Fund (CBF) and the Canada Council for the Arts, and the Province of British Columbia through the British Columbia Arts Council and the Book Publishing Tax Credit.

22 21 20 19 18  1 2 3 4 5

Printed in Canada

# Acknowledgements

**Gilakas'la.** I wish to gratefully acknowledge the former Chief of the 'Namgis First Nation, Kwaxalanukwa'me' 'Namugwis Bill Cranmer, and the 'Namgis Nation Council, 'Yalis (Alert Bay), home of the Killer Whale, for supporting my work over the past forty years. The Kwakwaka'wakw people, the Salmon People, have lived and thrived on the central BC coast since time immemorial. A very special thank you to Ga'axstalas Flora Cook, principal of the Alert Bay School, for her support and guidance over the years, and also to the Kwak'wala language and culture teachers for sharing their considerable knowledge and wisdom: 'Mam'xu'yugwa Auntie Ethel Alfred, Gwi'molas Vera Newman, Tłalilawikw Pauline Alfred, and Tidi Nelson. To 'Wadzidalaga Gloria Alfred, Gwixsisalas Emily Aitkin, 'Nalaga Donna Cranmer (principal of Wagalus School, Fort Rupert), 'Wełila'ogwa Irene Isaac (district principal of North Vancouver Island), Klaapalasugwela/Maxwagila Nella Nelson (Aboriginal Nations Education, Victoria School District), Mupenkin John Lyall (vice-principal of Edward Miln Secodary School, Sooke), Musgam'dzi Kaleb Child (Aboriginal Education, BC Ministry of Education), I wish to express my deep appreciation for their friendship and support. What has brought us together is our common love of family, the ocean, the seashore, and all plants, animals, and entities of our blue planet.

Through the character of Aunt Kate, a retired marine biologist, the children in this book explore basic marine ecology concepts. Through the words of Ada, the children experience a glimpse into an Indigenous view of knowledge and learning. The Elders teach that all plants and animals are connected and related. When we take care of nature, nature takes care of us. It is my hope that the adventures of Sam and Crystal will help children embrace all plants and animals as family.

Gilakas'la.

# A Wild and Beautiful Coastline

**E**arly in the morning on the first day of spring break, Crystal woke with a start. She raced downstairs to knock on her little brother's bedroom door.

"Get up, sleepy head!" she called. "We've got to get going if we want to catch Uncle Charlie's fishing boat. He said he's leaving at dawn, with or without us!"

Sam jumped out of bed like a bolt of lightning. He definitely didn't want to miss the boat!

The two children lived in Fisherman Bay, a small town famous for its halibut, salmon, and crab fishing. Today they would make the long voyage to Eagle Cove, where Uncle Charlie and Aunt Kate lived.

Aunt Kate was a retired marine biologist. She knew everything about the ocean and seashore life. In his younger days, Uncle Charlie had been one of the best fishermen on the coast. Nowadays, he mainly caught fish for himself and Aunt Kate—which was important because they live far, far away from the nearest grocery store!

The only way to get to Eagle Cove was to travel north by boat, because the coast was lined with steep mountains and there were no roads. The children were looking forward to a whole week of exploring tidal pools with Aunt Kate and listening to Uncle Charlie's tall fish tales.

After quickly washing up, and waking up their parents to say goodbye, Crystal and Sam slung on their backpacks and raced out the door.

"Remember to wear your lifejackets!" yelled their father after them. "And don't run around on the deck!"

"Be polite and helpful to your aunt and uncle!" called their mother. "And remember to have fun!"

**Sam and Crystal** walked briskly to the freshly painted red government dock, passing several fishing vessels. When they reached a seine boat with the words *Blue Heron* painted on its hull, they stopped. Uncle Charlie's head popped through the porthole.

"All aboard!" he said cheerfully. "Step lively!"

"There's a northeasterly wind blowing," came Aunt Kate's voice from somewhere inside the cabin. "We've got to motor if we want to reach home before dark."

The children hopped onboard and got settled. They hugged their aunt and uncle hello. Then they were on their way!

As soon as the *Blue Heron* left the protection of the harbour and the bay, the landscape changed. Rolling hills and gentle forests gave way to a wild and beautiful coastline. The children looked out the

porthole window to see steep rocky cliffs rising straight up from the crashing surf. A dark, thick forest of stunted trees crowded to the water's edge.

In the captain's cabin, Uncle Charlie stood at the wheel looking out the starboard window. From time to time, the children took turns steering the boat, but only in calm water. Uncle Charlie studied his map and electronic navigation equipment carefully to make sure the boat safely avoided the hundreds of hidden rocky reefs.

Many shipwrecks had occurred on this coastline, and hundreds of people had lost their lives.

"You can never be too cautious when it comes to the ocean," Uncle Charlie warned.

The ship's bell rang, signalling breakfast time. Inside the cabin, Aunt Kate placed a stack of fluffy blueberry pancakes on the table in front of a starving Sam and Crystal. The pancakes tasted so good with butter and syrup that the children forgot they were heading out to sea.

But outside, the sky grew dark and strong winds blew. The headwind grew stronger and stronger, and it pushed the old fishing boat sideways. Mountains of water splashed against the *Blue Heron's* bow. The children could hear the engine working harder and harder. **WHRRRRRR!** The pancakes and dishes slid back and forth on the table.

"It's getting rough," cautioned Aunt Kate. "We'd better clear the table and check that our lifejackets are zipped up tight."

Crystal started gathering up plates and carrying them to the sink when she noticed Sam hadn't moved from his chair.

"Come on, Sam!" She poked him in the ribs, before adding in a whisper, "Remember what Mom said when we were leaving?"

"I–I don't feel so good," said Sam weakly.

"Holy moly!" exclaimed his sister. "You're turning green!"

"Uh-oh. I think you're getting seasick," said Aunt Kate, clinging to the railing.

"Seasick?" asked Sam, alarmed. "Is there a cure?"

"Sitting on the deck in the fresh air usually helps," replied his aunt.

"Yikes!" said Crystal, trying to help Sam up the stairs as the boat rocked and rolled.

"Don't worry," said Aunt Kate. "Uncle Charlie's been in storms worse than this before. He'll keep us safe!"

# Flippers and Fins

To escape the violent surf near Devil's Nose Lighthouse, the *Blue Heron* veered northwest into the Pacific. At last the ocean calmed down, and the long swell lapped gently against the boat's hull. Sam returned to his normal colour and regained his spirits.

Crystal and Sam stood on the deck with binoculars, ready for action. They didn't have to wait long. In the distance, the sea churned crazily, tossing white water into the air.

"Holy smoke!" shouted Sam. "What's happening over there?"

"It's a pod of White-sided Dolphins!" yelled Aunt Kate over the noise of the surf. "There must be hundreds of them, and they're headed right for us!"

Before Sam could say "lickety-split," the dolphins had caught up with the *Blue Heron*. Several surfaced beside the boat and began riding the bow wave, leaping high out of the water and diving back into it. The agile animals performed a variety of acrobatics, including somersaults and belly flops, all the way to Agate Beach before heading out to sea.

"That was spectacular," exclaimed Crystal. "The dolphins are so beautiful. I love their colours—the dark grey on top and pale grey streak along each side."

"They're soooo fast," added Sam. "It's like they're dancing."

**Not far from** a rocky headland, the *Blue Heron* slowed to approach a half-exposed rocky reef. Several Harbour Seals rested like mermaids in deep water just offshore, their large brown eyes above water. As the boat drew near, they sank silently below the surface. Uncle Charlie steered as close as possible without disturbing the seals, while at the same time avoiding the dangerous submerged rocky reefs clearly marked by patches of Giant Kelp.

On land, the adult Harbour Seals basked on the sunlit rocks or perched on drift logs. Crystal remarked that they looked like over-stuffed sausages. The seal pups seemed unaware of the seine boat as they chased and rolled and squirmed about on their bellies. Underwater they propelled themselves forwards by their hind-flippers and used their small fore-flippers to steer. They were surprisingly quick.

"They're feeding on small fish called herring," said Aunt Kate. "They also eat crab, squid, and octopus."

Uncle Charlie slowly steered the seine boat past the rocky reefs and back out into open ocean. Then, to make up time, he travelled offshore at full speed in calm waters for more than an hour. As the seine boat neared the final rocky headland before White Sand Beach, they were met with a loud chorus of sharp, hoarse barking.

"That's the bark and roar of California Sea Lions," chuckled Aunt Kate. "The huge bulls can be heard from miles away."

Uncle Charlie slowed the engine and manoeuvred the boat as close to the rocks as possible while staying clear of submerged reefs. Hundreds of sea lions snuggled tightly together in sunning groups. Juveniles, or yearlings, wearing golden-chocolate coats, squirmed among the darker adults.

"Why are they fighting?" asked Sam, pointing at two fierce males. Facing each other, they had reared up on their fore-flippers and

galumphed along in a lunging, plunging gallop.

"The bulls battle each other for favoured beach territory and for the harems of ten or twelve females who give birth to their pups," explained Aunt Kate.

Several juvenile sea lions chased each other or pushed and shoved each other off the rocks. Other juveniles enjoyed playing in the water: body surfing, bubble chasing, kelp tossing, or shooting out of the water and flying through the air, dolphin-style, and in unison.

Aunt Kate got a serious "teacher" expression on her face. "Did you know that for many decades, there were very few sea lions and seals living in the wild on this coast?"

"Really? But we've seen so many of them today," said Crystal.

"That's because all marine mammals are now protected by law, and many populations have been increasing recently. But in the 1800s, European and Asian hunters were killing seals and sea lions by the thousands until they practically vanished."

"It's a good thing the hunting has stopped!" said Sam.

"Yes," agreed Aunt Kate. "But marine mammals are still in danger. Do you guys have any idea why?"

"Pollution," guessed Crystal, "like garbage and plastic floating in the ocean."

"Also, they eat fish," reasoned Sam, "so maybe if fishermen catch too many fish, the seals and sea lions could run out of food." He looked sheepishly at Uncle Charlie, hoping he hadn't offended all fishermen.

"You're both right," said Aunt Kate. "Also oil spills and warming ocean water threaten these remarkable, intelligent animals."

"Sea lions can be a nuisance for fishermen," chimed in Uncle Charlie. "I've seen them leap into fishing nets, gulp down salmon, and leap out again before the net is closed."

"Yes, but humans have to learn to live alongside our marine mammal friends," insisted Aunt Kate.

"Plus, the seals and sea lions were here first," added Crystal.

"You got that right," said Aunt Kate. "If humans make the right decisions, we can all live together."

# A Raucous
# Seabird Rookery

**A**s the *Blue Heron* approached White Sand Beach, the landscape changed dramatically. The sandy beach was a long white crescent laced with bubbling arches of foam. Wave after wave rolled gently against the sloping sandy bottom before losing momentum and breaking into surf as it reached shore.

"It's so beautiful," gasped Crystal.

"I love the ocean," said Aunt Kate. "I always feel happy and at peace when I travel along this sea coast."

As they neared Rocky Headlands, the landscape changed again. The long sandy beach ended abruptly where jagged coastal bluffs and haystack rocks fell into the ocean.

Sam stood on the deck, feet wide apart to steady himself, searching the horizon with his binoculars. He was hoping to spot Killer Whales, but instead he saw thousands and thousands of seabirds crowding the coastal bluffs and offshore islands. Uncle Charlie slowed the engine and steered the old seine boat towards the bluffs so they could get a better view.

First came the piercing symphony of high-pitched squawks and squeals. Then came the strong odours of rotting fish, decomposing seaweed, and seabird droppings.

"Ugh!" Sam and Crystal held their noses, but Uncle Charlie just chuckled. He was used to the smells of the sea.

"Life is abundant here," said Aunt Kate. "Otherwise all these seabirds could not survive and raise their young. The deep waters below teem with herring, cod, smelt, and other fish."

"Tufted Puffins at the top of the cliff!" yelled an ecstatic Crystal. "I've always wanted to see puffins."

At the top of the rock bluff Tufted Puffins nested in grass-lined burrows or in crevices. Hundreds and hundred of puffins stood close by their burrows on stout orange legs. With their short, stocky build they looked a bit like penguins. But their red-rimmed eyes, white face mask, large reddish-orange bill, and wind-blown straw-coloured head plumes also gave them a clownish look.

The short-winged puffins dropped from the cliff, free-falling until they gained enough momentum to take flight. Once airborne, they passed like flying torpedoes to and from their fishing grounds some distance offshore. On their return flight, they carried neat rows of slender fish, head to tail, in their bills—food for their young.

"I see hundreds of brown birds just below the puffins!" yelled Sam. "And hundreds of chicks too!"

Below the puffins, almost shoulder to shoulder among the highest rocks, clustered thousands of cliff-nesting Common Murres. The adults had sharp, pointed bills and short wings, with rich brownish black above and white below. Each nesting pair laid a single, pear-shaped egg on rocky ledges along sea cliffs. They turned their dark brown backs to the sea to protect their eggs and newly hatched chicks from predators.

**KERAWKK! KERAWK!** The parents signalled from below the ledges for the young chicks to leave their nest. One by one, several of those very little birds on those very high cliffs scrambled and tumbled down the cliffs, peeping excitedly all the way to the water. Miraculously, they were not hurt at all. Once in the water, they were met by their parents and escorted to the open sea.

The noisy Glaucous-winged Gulls settled under low salal bushes and in crevices lower on the cliff, or scattered among the murres. The gulls were easy to spot with their clean white head and pale grey mantle, yellowish bill, and flesh-coloured legs. They busily patrolled the cliff, waiting for an opportunity to snatch and steal. Although sharp-eyed and fiercely protective, the puffins and murres lost many eggs and young offspring to the hungry gulls.

The gulls' nests, made of rockweed or kelp, with feathers, sticks, and broken pieces of fish bones, were not much to look at, but they were always out of their neighbours' reach.

"I see their chicks," shouted Sam, pointing to a high ledge. "They're grey and sort of blend in with the rocks."

Sam and Crystal watched in amazement as the chicks aggressively followed their parents about with shoulders hunched forwards,

begging with an upward toss of the head and a whining, high-pitched **MEW! MEW!**

"Why are the chicks pecking at that red spot on their parents bill?" asked Sam. "Is it like a target?"

"Good observation," said Aunt Kate. "The red spot is indeed a target. The pecking triggers a response from the parents to cough up some food for the chicks."

Sam made a face, but Aunt Kate continued. "We are lucky to arrive here in April during the spring chick-rearing time. Three or four weeks from now many of these sea birds will have migrated."

# Sea Otter Nursery

**T**he *Blue Heron* continued north into the sun, with the wind at her back. Suddenly, an excited Uncle Charlie opened the wheelhouse window and yelled: "SEA OTTERS STRAIGHT AHEAD!" He killed the engine and allowed the boat to drift silently.

In the middle of a large kelp bed, several Sea Otters were sleeping or resting, all carefully wrapped up in the long glossy stems and fronds of kelp, as though they were in bed. The kelp anchored them to the sea bottom so they wouldn't float away. The otters were all lying on their backs with their heads sticking up and their paws together.

"*Sssshhh…*" whispered Sam. "We shouldn't wake them up."

The *Blue Heron* drifted until the children could hear grunts and growls coming from a very large kelp bed nearby. Before long, a nursery group of mother-and-pup pairs came into view. The pups nursed on rich warm milk from their mothers. While the pups nursed, the mothers groomed them, licking their fur and blowing to help it dry.

The pups were the noisiest otters. When a mother left her pup to look for food, the pup squealed, **WEE, WEE!**, like the cry of a gull, as if to say, "Where are you going, Mom? Feed me now!"

The Sea Otters at the edge of the nursery raft kept busy, somer-saulting and rolling, then slowly licking their paws, flippers, chest, and face—in that order.

"What are they doing?" asked Sam, puzzled.

"A Sea Otter spends much of its time grooming and cleaning its fur to maintain its special insulating qualities," explained Aunt Kate. "Sea Otters have very little blubber to keep them warm in a cold ocean. Instead they have dense, water-resistant fur to protect them against the chilly waters. When you see a Sea Otter somer-saulting and rubbing its body, it's not only cleaning its fur but also trapping air bubbles within the millions of tiny fur fibres. Their velvety fur is made up of two layers. The long outer guard hairs give the otter its soft and fuzzy appearance and keep the under-fur dry. Underneath the guard hairs is a layer of extremely fine and dense fur."

"The fuzzy pups look so cute and cuddly," said Crystal. "I'm glad there are lots of pups."

"I'm glad too," said Aunt Kate. "There was a time not long ago when Sea Otters went extinct along this coastline.

"What do you mean extinct?" asked Sam.

"Extinct means that there were no Sea Otters living on this coast," said Crystal, recalling her school science class.

"Hundreds of thousands of Sea Otters once lived along the North Pacific coast," said Aunt Kate. "For centuries the Indigenous Peoples

hunted Sea Otters for their fur, but they never took so many that they caused the population to become endangered.

"Then, between the 1700s and the early 1900s, fur traders from Europe and Asia killed every sea otter they could find. Sea otters are slow swimmers because they feed on slow-moving prey such as sea urchins, abalone, crabs, octopus, and clams. So they were no match for speedy boats and guns. All but a few Sea Otters in this region were killed. Then, from 1969 to 1972, marine scientists moved a few small groups of Sea Otters from Alaska south to this area of the Pacific Northwest coast, and their numbers have been slowly growing ever since."

"It's scary to think that Sea Otters were once extinct on this coast," said Crystal.

"Yes, very scary. Even today, one oil spill in the wrong place could wipe out an entire population. But there is an army of folks along this

coast and worldwide who care deeply about wildlife and who are working together to make a difference. As long as we make the right decisions, the ocean will remain rich with life."

"That makes me feel a whole lot better," said Crystal.

"Me too," added Sam.

Uncle Charlie started the motor, reversed engines, and slowly steered the *Blue Heron* away from the Sea Otter nursery, then picked up speed and headed north.

"If only I could see Killer Whales," pleaded Sam. "They're so powerful and sleek. It would make a perfect day."

"You never know when you're going to see Killer Whales," said Uncle Charlie. "It could happen at any moment, or you could wait and wait and wait for a very long time."

Sam stood on the deck as the seine boat pitched to and fro, binoculars ready for action.

# Eagle Cove

**T**he rest of the trip seemed to take forever. Then the winds died down and the landscape changed once again. At last they could make out the dark tones of the rocky shore of Eagle Cove. The offshore islands and several haystack rocks created a protected cove and provided shelter from storms and high waves. An evergreen forest of cedar, fir, spruce, and pine trees covered the landscape. Unlike the stunted, twisted trees that crowded the coastal bluffs along the windswept coast, the trees here stood tall and straight right down to the water's edge.

As the *Blue Heron* neared the entrance to the cove, a majestic bird with a white head and tail, a hooked yellow bill, and a dark brown body circled and skimmed the surface of the water looking for prey. The Bald Eagle swooped down and snatched a salmon swimming near the surface. With amazing strength it flew, holding the salmon in its golden talons to gain altitude. The eagle let out a high-pitched squeaky call: **KLEEK-KIT-IK-IK-IK.**

"Wow! Incredible!" exclaimed Sam. "The salmon must weigh as much as the eagle."

The eagle glanced down with piercing yellow eyes as it beat against the same wind as the *Blue Heron*, towards a common destination. The eagle easily pulled away on strong, steady wing beats. Then it spread its wings wide and landed in a huge bowl-shaped nest at the top of a tall dead cedar tree.

"Look! Look!" yelled Sam peering through his binoculars. "A baby eagle. It's all fluffy and grey!"

"Good eye," said Aunt Kate. "Gradually feathers will replace the grey fluffy down. The parents take turns staying on the nest until the eggs are hatched and the young are several weeks old. They protect the chicks from ravens and gulls that will break open eggs or steal the young."

**Once they were** inside the cove, the water was perfectly calm. The old house stood on a boulder bluff overlooking the cove. Uncle Charlie had installed porthole windows, which provided a perfect view of the shoreline below, and solar heating panels on the roof.

Uncle Charlie slowed the engine and steered the seine boat alongside the wooden dock. On the shore at the low-tide level was a woman picking paper-thin blackish seaweed from the rocks and putting it into a bucket. The woman waved and Aunt Kate waved back. Then the woman picked up a drum and began singing a welcome song: "Heeya, Heeya, Heeya Hey!"

The woman held her drum in one hand and picked up the bucket of seaweed with her other hand and walked quickly to greet the incoming boat.

"Welcome home, my friends," she called cheerfully. "I was beginning to get worried."

Aunt Kate introduced the woman to the children. "This is my good friend Ada. She's teaching me the traditional Indigenous way to dry seaweed."

"Would you like to taste some?" offered Ada.

"No thanks," said Sam. He couldn't imagine eating black icky seaweed.

"Maybe later," Crystal added, trying to be polite.

Uncle Charlie finished tying the seine boat to the dock and said, "Okay, guys. Take your packsacks and some of the groceries up to the house. I'll bring the rest."

Crystal and Sam collected their belongings and began the long walk from the wooden dock to the house. They walked past several crab traps and an old fishing net and went up the stairs towards the house. When they reached the top of the stairs that led to the house, Aunt Kate and Uncle Charlie gave the children a tour. Ada joined them.

Behind the house where strong winds often blew stood Uncle Charlie's pride and joy: a windmill, which generated electricity. A small greenhouse for growing vegetables was tucked against the south side of the house, along with wooden racks covered with seaweed.

"If we can get a few days of good hot weather, the sun will dry the seaweed," said Aunt Kate. "Then we can eat it anytime we want and I'll be able to use it in my cooking over the winter. It adds good flavour to soups and chowders."

Sam and Crystal exchanged nervous glances. They realized they would have to taste seaweed sooner or later during this visit.

"We're adding seaweed to the vegetable garden," continued Aunt Kate. "Seaweeds are bursting with minerals, and they add nutrients to the soil and make the seeds sprout faster and the vegetables grow better."

needles grow in pairs

mature cone

Shore Pine

cone

flat branches with scale-like leaves ~ tiny cones

Western Red Cedar

flat, one-inch needles

young cones

mature cone

Douglas Fir

Sitka Spruce

flattish, very sharp needles

Growing in humid coastal forest.

Growing in the open

Adding seaweed to a vegetable garden didn't make much sense to Sam, but he nodded his head anyway.

A small smokehouse built with cedar wood stood on the shore well above the tide line. Smoke gently billowed from under its roof.

"Ada kept a low fire going while we went south to pick you guys up," said Aunt Kate. "We're smoking Sockeye Salmon, my favourite!"

No sooner had the words been spoken than a small slender dark brown animal with short legs and a bushy tail ran from the smoke-house with a half-eaten salmon in its mouth.

Seaweed Drying Rack

"YOU MISCHIEVOUS RASCAL!" yelled Uncle Charlie. He grabbed a bamboo rake and chased after it. "GET! SHOO! SCOOT! THAT'S MY SALMON!"

The little mink was fast and nimble. It ran with its half-eaten lunch in its mouth down the stairs from the house, under the dock, and along the beach, where it disappeared between dark boulders.

Wind Vane

"Clever mink," chuckled Aunt Kate. "We thought we'd made the smokehouse animal proof!"

"It's a pretty little animal," admired Crystal, while Uncle Charlie fumed over his lost salmon.

Ada smiled. "I should get home before it gets dark," she said.

"Where do you live?" asked Crystal.

"In Salmon Bay Village," she replied. "I'll be back in a few days to check on the seaweed and maybe join you for a cup of tea."

Solar Panels

They said their goodbyes and waved as Ada went down to the dock, got into her aluminum boat, and started the motor. The children watched as the motorboat and Ada got smaller and smaller in the distance.

Tomorrow, Aunt Kate would take the two children on a beach walk to explore the tidal pools high on the shore. Sam and Crystal could hardly wait. Aunt Kate knew every tidal pool and every creature on the seashore. She seemed to know everything there was to know about the ocean.

greenhouse

Smoke House

Fire Box

# The Trouble with Tides

The sun was high in the sky when Crystal and Sam met Aunt Kate on the shore. They were excited to explore the seashore critters that live in the beautiful tidal pools low on the shore. But there was one great big problem.

"Oh, no!" exclaimed Crystal. "What's wrong? Why is the tide so high?"

Only barren rocks and a few small tidal pools were visible high on the shore.

"This is crazy," added Sam. "Last time we were here, the tide was way out."

"I'm afraid this is as low as the tide will get today," said Aunt Kate. "But there are plenty of interesting critters to see this high on the shore."

"But I wanted to see a Sunflower Sea Star, the kind that looks like a sunburst." Crystal couldn't hide her disappointment.

"I wanted to see prickly sea urchins," complained Sam, "and a Giant Pacific Octopus."

"Here's a puzzle for you both," said Aunt Kate. "If you were a snail, a crab, or a sea star, what is the most important event that happens at the seashore?"

Sam and Crystal looked at her blankly, still thinking about the creatures they wouldn't be seeing that day.

"It's an event that determines when you eat, whether you can move or not, where you live on the shore, and it can even determine whether you live or die," Aunt Kate continued. "I should add that it's an event that usually happens twice a day."

"Is it the tide?" guessed Sam.

"That's right! The level of the sea is always changing. Twice each day seawater rises up the shore and creeps upon the land, and then flows back out to sea again. That movement of water up and down is called the tide. Twice each day the animals and plants are covered with salty seawater and then exposed to air, and sometimes to the drying effects of the wind and sun."

"But how does the tide affect where on the shore seashore plants and animals live?" asked Crystal.

"Animals are pretty smart," Aunt Kate explained. "You see, the seashore is divided into zones according the length of time each zone is covered by seawater or exposed to air. Scientists call these four zones the Spray Zone, High Tide Zone, Middle Tide Zone, and Low Tide Zone."

"So the seaweeds and animals that live in the Spray Zone are different from the animals that live in the Low Tide Zone?" asked Crystal.

"Exactly! I think of the collections of seaweeds and animals as communities, and the communities of seaweeds and animals in each tide zone are different because the conditions for life are different."

# Tidal Zone Organisms

[1]  Black Lichens

[2]  Periwinkles

[3]  Small Acorn Barnacles

[4]  Rock Louse

[5]  Finger Limpets

[6]  Purple Shore Crab

[7]  Thatched Acorn Barnacles

[8]  Sea Lettuce

[9]  Black Chiton

[10]  Rockweeds

[11]  Hairy Hermit Crab

[12]  Tidepool Sculpin

[13]  Pink-tipped Sea Anemones

[14]  Sea Sac

[15]  Red Rock Crab

[16]  Surf Grass

[17]  California Blue Mussels

[18]  Wrinkled Whelks with Egg Cases

[19]  Purple or Ochre Sea Stars

[20]  Giant Green Sea Anemones

[21]  Goose Neck Barnacles

[22]  Lined Chiton

[23]  Keyhole Limpets

[24]  Coon-striped Shrimp

[25]  Decorator Crab

[26]  Opalescent Nudibranch

[27]  Giant Red Sea Urchins

[28]  Sunflower Sea Star

[29]  Pink Encrusting Coral Seaweed

[30]  Giant Pacific Octopus

"So it's like a high-rise apartment building with many storeys, one above the other," said Crystal.

"That's a great comparison! And the collection of seashore critters on each floor is somewhat different. At first it seems complicated, but it really isn't. When you are more familiar with the seaweeds and animals and where they are located on the shore, the tide zones will make more sense."

The children were still a bit disappointed that the tide had ruined their chances of seeing a Sunflower Sea Star and a Giant Pacific Octopus, but they perked right up when Aunt Kate said, "It must be time for a nice cup of hot chocolate and huckleberry muffins."

# Mother Rock Louse Has Babies

**T**he rocks high on the shore appeared empty and lifeless. All Sam and Crystal could see were body parts—broken crab shells and crab legs, empty clam and mussel shells, empty snail shells, and broken sea urchin shells.

*How can Aunt Kate be excited about exploring such a boring place?* thought Sam. He wanted to go lower on the shore, closer to the water.

"This is a mystery," said Aunt Kate. "Why do you think there are broken shells this high on the shore?"

Crystal thought for a moment before saying, "I've seen crows and seagulls eat mussels and leave behind broken shells."

"And what about River Otters?" added Sam. "They could sure make a mess on the beach."

Aunt Kate chuckled. "Now you're getting the idea."

Suddenly a strange creature like a large wood bug scurried over the rocks.

"That Rock Louse is a beauty," exclaimed Aunt Kate. "Catch it if you can!"

The Rock Louse led the two children on a merry chase over the rocks until Crystal captured it in a crevice.

"Turn it upside down," said Aunt Kate, "and you might discover something quite wonderful."

Crystal turned the animal over and discovered about thirty tiny baby animals clinging to the underside of the mother's body.

"Cool," said Crystal, "Look how the mother rolls up into a round ball to protect herself."

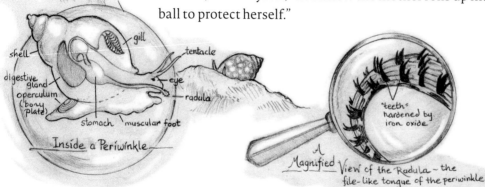

Sitka periwinkles

checkered periwinkles

shell
digestive gland
operculum ("bony plate")
gill
tentacle
eye
radula
stomach    muscular foot

Inside a Periwinkle

"teeth" hardened by iron oxide

A Magnified View of the Radula ~ the file-like tongue of the periwinkle

"Usually the Rock Louse comes out only at night to feed on seaweed and stays high on the shore. In fact, you might think it's afraid of getting its feet wet. Let's search in the crevices to see if we can find a very small snail called a periwinkle."

Sam and Crystal looked all over the rocks but couldn't see a single living thing.

"Where?" asked Sam. "I don't see any snails."

"Look again," said Aunt Kate. "Train your eyes to see these soft brown or dull grey animals."

After a while Sam said, "I see one! And there's another one."

Crystal joined in. "I see lots on the rocks, and there's more in this crevice here."

"Holy smoke!" said Sam. "There must be hundreds . . . no thousands . . . no *millions* of periwinkles."

Aunt Kate looked pleased.

"These little snails must be pretty tough to live this high on the shore," said Sam.

"That's right," said Aunt Kate. "Look closely and you will see a hard bony plate at the tip of the snail's foot, called an operculum (*o-per-cu-lum*). It acts like a door, sealing the snail's soft body inside, keeping the wetness in until the tide returns."

"What do the periwinkles eat?" asked a puzzled Crystal. "All I see is rocks."

"They scrape the rocks to feed on tiny plant-like black lichens (*li-kans*)," explained Aunt Kate. "Lichens cover the rocks high on the shore and look like a black stain."

"But how do the periwinkles feed on such tiny food?" wondered Sam.

"Snails have a very long, thin, ribbon-like tongue called a radula (*rad-u-la*)," said Aunt Kate. "The radula has many rows of small, sharp, curved teeth like sandpaper. Snails scrape the rocks with their radula to feed on the lichens."

"Cool," said Sam.

"Now look closely in spray pools and in moist crevices on the rocks and you will see small white Acorn Barnacles," continued Aunt Kate. "A barnacle is cemented to a rock by part of its head, and it strains its food from the water with its feet. It's an upside-down animal."

Lichen

finger Limpets

home-spot scar

Underside of a Limpet

mouth

flat muscular foot

eating scars

Speckled Limpets

The children found lots of barnacles, along with little armies of small, brown, cone-shaped animals scattered on dry rocks.

"Those are limpets," said Aunt Kate.

"They're stuck on tight like cement," exclaimed Sam, trying to pry one off.

"When out of seawater, a limpet uses its large muscular foot to create a powerful suction to hold onto rocks. Why do you think they clamp so hard onto the rocks?"

Sam thought for a moment. "To be safe from predators?"

"That's one reason. Can you think of another, Crystal? Think about survival in the Spray Zone."

"I know!" said Crystal. "It's like the periwinkle with the little door at the tip of its foot. It keeps the shell-house moist to protect the limpet from drying out in the hot sun."

That was the answer Aunt Kate was looking for. "I have such a smart niece and nephew," she said proudly.

Aunt Kate found a small spray pool and invited the children to look for signs of life. On the bottom of the pool the cone-shaped limpets and periwinkles glided along on their wide muscular foot, grazing on black lichens and the thin film of slimy green algae that covered the rocks.

"Whoa!" cried Sam. "The barnacles have long feathery legs flickering in and out, like a fisherman's net. They must be feeding on something in the water, but I can't see what."

"The barnacles are using their legs to rake microscopic soup from the seawater. The plants and animals living this high on the shore have a harsh life. While the tide is out they must survive the hot sun. The pool starts to evaporate in the heat. It becomes warmer and saltier, and there is less oxygen for the animals. Nevertheless, the animals and plants living in the Spray Pool keep moist waiting for the sea to return."

"Wow," said Crystal. "Who would have thought there would be so many interesting animals among these rocks?"

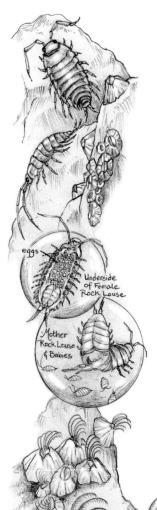

eggs

Underside of Female Rock Louse

Mother Rock Louse & Babies

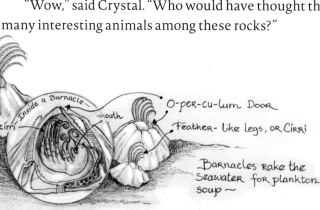

cirri  Inside a Barnacle  mouth  O-per-cu-lum Door

Feather-like legs, or Cirri

Barnacles rake the seawater for plankton soup ~

# Tasty Plankton Soup

**T**he next morning Sam and Crystal met a cheerful Aunt Kate on the dock.

"Today you'll meet the fascinating tiny plants and animals that make up the drifting plankton. We'll drop a plankton net over the side of the dock and then walk along, dragging it behind. The net is made of very fine cloth and allows the seawater to flow through it, trapping tiny plants and animals in a collecting jar."

The two children took turns dragging the net back and forth through the water before pulling it up onto the dock. They peered into the collecting jar and saw tiny creatures the size of pencil dots darting here and there. Aunt Kate led the two children into the kitchen, which had been transformed into a science lab.

Aunt Kate dipped a medicine dropper into the jar of plankton. She carefully placed one drop of seawater onto a glass slide, placed the slide under the viewfinder of the microscope, and adjusted the lens until she got a clear image of the plankton.

When Crystal looked into the viewfinder, she was astonished to see tiny golden glass boxes and beautifully crafted wheels. Red, green, blue, and brown jewels floated in and out of view.

"Wow!" shouted Sam. "Some look like spaceships—and there's a lunar landing craft!"

Diatoms

Male Copepod

Female Copepod with Egg sacs

Female Amphipod with Egg sac

Male Amphipod

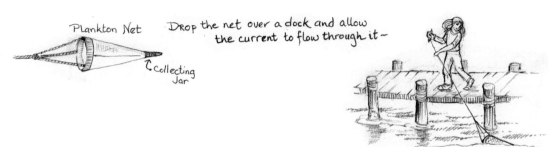
Plankton Net

Drop the net over a dock and allow the current to flow through it ~

Collecting Jar

"These sea vegetables are called diatoms. Each living diatom is a single-celled algae. Hundreds of diatoms can fit into a drop of seawater."

"Why do they sparkle?" asked Crystal.

"Each golden diatom cell is contained inside a glass shell," explained Aunt Kate. Each time the children looked into the view-finder, they could hardly believe their eyes.

Use a medicine dropper to catch the plankton

"There's a creature with one big red eye and two swishing long antennae!" exclaimed Crystal.

"That's a copepod (co-pe-pod), one of the most common types of animal plankton," said Aunt Kate. "They float in the ocean all their lives, from egg to adult."

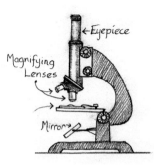
← Eyepiece
Magnifying Lenses
Mirror

"I see one that looks like a dragon!" shrieked Sam. "It has big black eyes, a long sharp horn, and a feathery tail."

"What you're seeing is a teeny-tiny baby crab," laughed Aunt Kate.

"You're kidding!" said Sam, surprised. "It doesn't look anything like a crab."

"It doesn't look like a crab now, but the baby crab hatched from an egg the size of a pinhead and will change its shape many times as it grows. Most seashore creatures —including sea stars, snails, crabs, barnacles, clams, shrimp, and sea urchins— spend the first stages of their lives floating in the ocean as larvae."

Prepare a slide

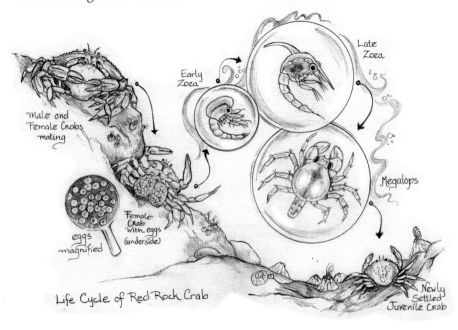

Male and Female Crabs mating

Early Zoea

Late Zoea

Megalops

eggs magnified

Female Crab with eggs (underside)

Newly Settled Juvenile Crab

Life Cycle of Red Rock Crab

"It's like how caterpillars turn into butterflies," added Crystal. "We learned about metamorphosis in school."

"That's right," said Aunt Kate. "The baby crabs, barnacles, and sea stars spend the first part of their lives drifting with the ocean current before they get large enough to sink to the bottom and begin life as bottom dwellers. Although most plankton animals are in the seawater all their lives, the larvae are there only for a while."

"So this is what the barnacles are eating—tiny diatoms and tiny animal plankton?" asked Crystal.

"Exactly. The larger animal plankton eat smaller animal plankton, and the copepods eat diatoms."

"Where do the diatoms get their food?" asked Sam.

"They drift near the surface of the sea and use sunlight to make food, just like plants do on land," explained Aunt Kate. "It's an amazing process called photosynthesis."

"Photo-what?" asked Sam, looking confused.

Aunt Kate smiled. "All you need to remember is that seawater is a mixture of diatoms and tiny animal plankton. Waves churn dead and decaying animals and seaweeds into tiny shreds of food that float in the seawater. The diatoms, animal plankton, and shreds of food become a sort of plankton soup. Many larger animals, like barnacles and mussels, feed on plankton. Larger animals feed on barnacles and mussels. It's an endless food chain."

"Being salty seawater, the soup is seasoned just right," joked Sam.

"Speaking of soup," said Aunt Kate, "it's almost dinner time. How about some delicious clam chowder?"

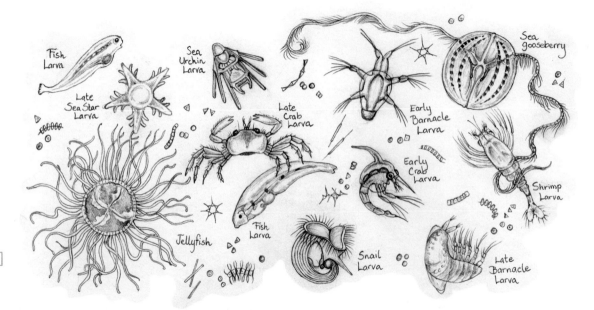

Fish Larva

Late Sea Star Larva

Sea Urchin Larva

Late Crab Larva

Early Barnacle Larva

Sea gooseberry

Early Crab Larva

Shrimp Larva

Jellyfish

Fish Larva

Snail Larva

Late Barnacle Larva

# Crusty Crabs and
# Flipping Fish

The next morning when they reached the shore for the day's exploration, Aunt Kate took the map of the seashore from her backpack and pointed to the High Tide Zone.

"Today we're exploring an area that is normally uncovered, except during high tides. Like the Spray Zone, the animals that live here are more used to air than to seawater, but the High Tide Zone has a greater variety of seaweeds and animals.

Eager to see what critters lived in the High Tide Zone, Crystal turned over one of the cobblestones, taking care not to crush any animals in the process. To her delight, several Purple Shore Crabs scuttled sideways from their hiding places before disappearing under nearby rocks. Then she saw an eel-like fish wiggle and flip, slither and slide, and slip under a nearby rock. She let out a shriek just as Sam cried out, "Electric eel!"

Aunt Kate chuckled. "The long dorsal fin makes it look like an eel, but don't worry, you two. It's just a blenny—a perfectly harmless fish."

Relieved, Sam and Crystal went back to exploring the High Tide Zone. They were surprised to see the collection of animals attached to the underside of the rock: flat worms, tiny tubeworms, and clear, jelly-like masses of eggs.

"How did eggs get here?" asked Sam.

"Many fish swim into shallow water and lay their eggs in crevices and in hollows under rocks," explained Aunt Kate.

"So these eggs will hatch, and the tiny baby fish will swim into the sea and become part of the plankton?" asked Crystal.

antennae

gill slit

Purple Shore Crab
Female

eye stalk

"U" shaped Abdomen

Close-up of Mouth Parts

Young Purple Shore Crabs come in great varieties of colors and patterns

"That's right," answered Aunt Kate. "What do you think would happen if we turned the cobblestone upside down and left it there?"

"It would be like a giant turning your house upside down," said Crystal. "We might be killing the shore crabs and blennies and all the fish eggs and other animals that couldn't survive in the hot sun. A shore crab or fish in the open would be easy prey for hungry shore birds."

"You're beginning to understand the ways of the seashore," smiled Aunt Kate. Carefully, they turned the cobblestone right side up.

"Because crabs are so alert," continued Aunt Kate, "you might walk past dozens and not see them. They scuttle out of sight before you get near them." She suggested the children find a viewing spot among the boulders overlooking a tidal pool and be very quiet and still. "If you look and listen, nature will come to you."

Sam and Crystal walked in separate directions, looking for a good viewing spot. Sam sat on a boulder overlooking a tidal pool. He heard the Purple Shore Crabs scurrying around and out of sight, their hard crusty shells scraping the rocks. It didn't take long before he saw a claw poke out from under a rock, then two eyes and a second claw. Finally a whole crab appeared. Soon he saw them everywhere.

Sam didn't know it, but the crabs belonged to a group of organisms called arthropods (*ar-thro-pods*), which means "jointed legs." The crabs' legs and thin, flat body allowed them to crawl into cracks or skitter sideways among the rocks.

Sam watched the crab nearest him. It explored with its claws and feelers, or antennae, then munched on bright green Sea Lettuce. It used its small front claws for eating. Left, right, left, right—each claw in turn moved up to its mouth and down again, as if keeping time to fast music. Other crabs munched on the body parts of dead and decaying animals.

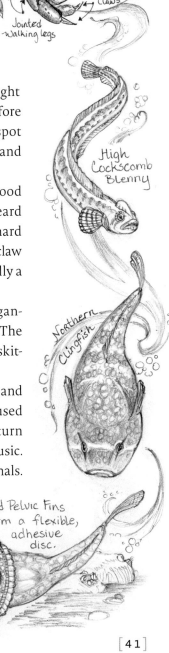

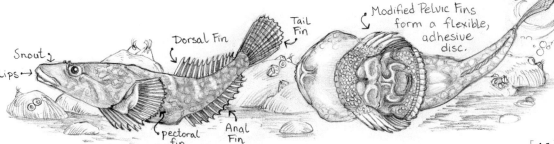

Crystal explored in the opposite direction and decided to turn over some rocks to see if she could find more shore crabs. It wasn't long before she turned over a rock to find a little fish with a large flat head clinging stubbornly to the underside of the rock. She had never seen a fish hold onto a rock before. With a start, she realized what it must be.

"Yuck! Aunt Kate, I found a bloodsucker!"

Aunt Kate and Sam came over to investigate. When Aunt Kate saw the little fish, she laughed.

"This is a Northern Clingfish, one of my favourite seashore critters. It slithers over wet rocks and clings to the underside of rocks with its special fins. The fins form a powerful suction device, but it is really a harmless fish."

"Why does it need a suction device?" Crystal shuddered, still thinking of the creature sucking her blood.

"Good question," said Aunt Kate. "When the tide goes out, the clingfish hold onto the rocks while the water washes out to sea. As long as blennies and clingfish have the protection of their under-rock habitat, they can survive until the incoming tide."

Crystal looked at the little fish again, and suddenly it didn't seem so creepy.

"We'd better turn the cobblestone right side up so that the animals on top don't dry up and die before the tide returns," she said.

"Or get eaten by hungry shore birds," added Sam.

"Great idea," said a very pleased Aunt Kate.

Underside of Cobblestone Hotel

Rockweed · Limpet · Acorn Barnacles · Tiny Tube Worms · Fish Eggs · Flatworm · Purple Shore Crab · Blenny · Nemertean Worm

*Make sure the former owner is out...*

# Two-fisted Hermit Crabs

*...Look it over*

*inside and Out...*

*Hop quickly, tail-first...*

*...into new shell home...*

*...make sure it's the right size.*

Crystal found a small tidal pool in the High Tide Zone. She sat down on a rock and put her face directly over the pool. The water was surprisingly clear. Rockweeds lined the walls and cast deep shadows. One snail shell caught Crystal's eye. It was a shiny black turban shell, its top worn by the surf to a pearly white reflecting the colours of the rainbow.

Crystal wasn't the only admirer of the empty shell. A large Hairy Hermit Crab had its eyes on it too. The hermit was dressed in a lovely horn shell, but the shell was too small to cover its soft abdomen. The hermit went from one empty snail shell to the next, grasping the wide opening and inspecting each one, as if shopping for a new coat. It twisted and turned each shell, tapping it with its long antennae, and reaching its arm up inside.

"What is the crab doing?" asked Crystal.

"Exactly what all hermit crabs do," said Aunt Kate. "Carrying a borrowed empty snail shell everywhere it goes. Its abdomen is curled to fit perfectly inside the spiral snail shell."

"But why does it carry a snail shell?"

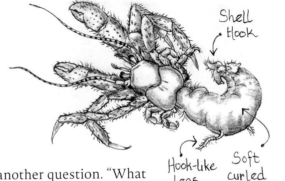

Shell
hook

Hook-like
legs

Soft
curled
abdomen

Aunt Kate answered her question with another question. "What do you think?"

"Hmmm . . ." Crystal thought for a moment. "Maybe if the hermit is threatened by a predator, like a fish with big teeth, it could pull itself inside its shell and use its large claw like a door to block the shell's opening."

"Right," said Aunt Kate. "Plus, by pulling its tender abdomen inside the shell and blocking the opening with its claws, it can keep the wetness inside at low tide and keep from drying out."

"Look!" yelled Sam. "I think we're about to see a fight!"

Just when the first hermit was half out of his shell to test the new one, a second Hairy Hermit Crab appeared from behind the thick curtains of Sea Lettuce. They had both settled on the same shell. Now the two big hermit crabs faced each other, legs spread apart, feelers waving and sensing the water. They stood with their powerful pinchers raised high. Their tender bodies were curled inside their snail shells, as if they were wearing padded boxing shorts. They lunged forward, swinging their pinchers like over-stuffed boxing gloves. A hook to the right, a jab to the left! Mud clouds mixed with shredded bits of Sea Lettuce rose and drifted off in a watery haze. The first hermit held the second in a hammerlock, and they tumbled over and over together until the second hermit was whirled smack into a boulder. Dazed, it rose slowly and staggered, feelers trembling but gloves still swinging. Then suddenly, the first hermit crab ran to the empty black turban shell, hopped out of its old shell and into the new shell, and ran off with it.

"Wow, what a fight!" cried Sam.

**Just below the** hermits' boxing ring, Crystal watched a beautiful flower garden unfold right before her eyes. She realized the flowers she was looking at were actually animals. When folded up, the Pink-tipped Sea Anemones were pale green, but when opened they revealed a ring of tentacles with delicate pink tips that swayed gently in the water, giving the appearance of flowers.

Reproduction by Budding

Broken fragments of body tissue

Each fragment can grow into an adult

Reproduction by Fission

"This is strange," she said. "One of the sea-flowers is pulling itself apart into two halves!"

"My, you are a good observer to see such a wonderful event!" praised Aunt Kate. "Many sea anemones reproduce by splitting themselves apart, dividing down the centre of the body, creating two identical twins, or clones."

Crystal could hardly believe her ears. Identical sea anemone twins!

"Some of the most fascinating battles fought in tidal pools are between clusters of clones," continued Aunt Kate. "Think of one cluster as one super family, all identical twins. For anemones that live high on the shore, this clustering reduces water loss. But when clones from one clan bump into clones of a different clan, that means war! The threatened sea anemones fire stinging poisonous darts stored in their tentacles at one another. The injured sea anemones retreat, leaving a narrow anemone-free battleground between the clashing armies."

Sam laughed. "Sounds like an action movie!"

Aunt Kate smiled. "This is one of the many ways seashore animals compete and battle for food and homes in a very crowded world."

A Sea Anemone can split itself into identical twins (clones)

The two armies, or clans, are separated by an anemone-free battleground.

# Tidepool Sculpins and Greedy Gulls

Black Chiton

Mossy Chiton

underside

Mouth
Mantle
Girdle
Muscular Foot
Anus

**S**am sat on a cedar log above the High Tide Zone scanning the horizon with his binoculars. He was searching for signs of Killer Whales: a whale breaching out of the water, a spout of mist from a blowhole, perhaps a tail fin. So far there was nothing.

Sensing Sam's frustration, Aunt Kate invited him and Crystal to sit quietly in the High Tide Zone overlooking a tidal pool. "You will be surprised at the amazing critters you will find, even in the smallest tidal pools, if you are very still," she whispered.

Gradually, animals ventured out from beneath the rocks and shadows of the pool. At the bottom of the pool, Kelp Fleas busily darted here and there to feast on seaweed and decaying animal matter. Both children thought all the bumps on the rocks were limpets, but now they noticed a large black one that was different. Like the limpets, this Black Chiton (ky-ton) had an armoured body and a flat muscular foot by which it clung stubbornly to rocks. Its shell was divided into eight bony plates held together by a tough leather-like girdle. It had probably been pulled from the rocks by a gull, the soft muscular foot and body parts eaten for breakfast. It lay curled up, all orange inside.

Several small fish glided from rock to rock. Once on the sandy bottom, they spread their forward fins wide and appeared to "walk" on their fins.

"These little fish sure have big heads and fins for the size of their bodies," laughed Sam.

"Those are Tidepool Sculpins," said Aunt Kate. "They use their teeth and powerful jaws to crush food items that have hard outside shells, like small barnacles or dead crabs, and eat the soft flesh inside.

"Butterfly Shell" found on the beach after the chiton dies

when forced from a rock, chitons curl up for protection

Topside

Shell
Mantle

But most of the time they are scavengers, like Kelp Fleas and crabs. They eat dead and decaying seaweed and animals."

Just as Sam was getting interested in Tidepool Sculpins, a hungry Glaucous-winged Gull appeared, flipping a bright Purple Sea Star upside down. The gull pecked and pecked at the underside of the sea star with its long sharp bill until there were no tube feet left. Then it picked up the sea star, shook it violently and smashed it against the rocks, again and again.

"Poor sea star!" cried Crystal.

Sam picked up a rock to throw at the gull, but Aunt Kate stopped him.

"Sometimes nature seems cruel, but this is its way. Every creature must eat. Let's sit quietly and see what happens next."

Crystal and Sam watched in disbelief as the gull slowly, very slowly, sucked one arm of the sea star and then another, into its mouth before slowly swallowing the animal whole.

"Yuck! Gives me the willies," Crystal grimaced. "But how can a gull swallow such a big sea star? It's a whole lot bigger than the seagull's mouth."

"Gulls have special juices in their mouth that makes the bony skin of the sea star soft, and they can unhinge their jaws to swallow large prey," explained Aunt Kate. "They will eat anything they can get, living or dead—snails, crabs, mussels, small clams, a variety of fish, even jellyfish."

"That's cool," said Sam, looking at the gull with newfound respect.

"So as you can see, the seashore is filled with adventure, even when there isn't a good low tide," said Aunt Kate. "The Middle Tide Zone and the Low Tide Zone are crowded with many interesting animals. Unfortunately, we can't explore the lower zones because each day over the next week the tide will be higher on the shore. Then, as the full moon approaches, the tides will go out lower on the shore."

Kelp Fleas leap to feast on decaying seaweeds & animals

Crystal looked worried. "So when is the best time to explore the Low Tide Zone?"

"The Low Tide Zone is only out of seawater for a few hours each day for four or five days each month at full moon."

"So, are you saying that the tide won't be low enough to explore the Low Tide Zone until after we go back home?"

"Sadly, yes," said Aunt Kate. "But if you come back over summer vacation, there will be several very low tides that occur during the day. We can explore them then."

Disappointed, Sam and Crystal walked slowly back along the shore. Crystal wanted to find more sea stars and sea anemones. Sam wanted to find sea urchins and maybe even an octopus.

"Tomorrow we'll have a picnic overlooking the sea," said Aunt Kate, trying to cheer them up. "I'll invite Ada. She makes the best stinging nettle tea. We'll have fish soup and seaweed chips and many seashore delights."

"What about just plain peanut butter cookies?" said Sam glumly.

Many kinds of Wild Berries make delicious jams, jellies, & teas

Salal

Oregon Grape

Stinging Nettle (tea)

Trailing Wild Blackberry

Sea Asparagus (salads)

# Picnic at Cedar Tree Lookout

The next morning the children woke suddenly to the *Blue Heron's* bell ringing. **CLANG, CLANG, CLANG!**

"Time to get up," sang Aunt Kate. "We're having breakfast at Cedar Tree Lookout."

"We're having breakfast in a *tree?*" yawned Sam.

"Aunt Kate has the craziest ideas," shrugged Crystal.

No sooner had the children met Uncle Charlie and Aunt Kate downstairs than they were out the door and walking through a forest of tall Red Cedar trees, Shore Pines, ferns, and wild flowers. As they neared the sea cliff, they saw Ada standing under a huge old cedar tree. She had built a fire and was stirring a pot of tender stinging nettle leaves and licorice fern roots to make tea. A few feet away from the pot, under the shade of the cedar tree, were a wooden table and chairs made of tree stumps. Ada gave Aunt Kate a hug. Then she welcomed Crystal, Sam, and Uncle Charlie to Cedar Tree Lookout. It was clear to the children that this was a special place.

Aunt Kate and Ada took several mysterious packages from their backpacks. Each package contained a special treat. Ada showed the children how to make a type of bread called bannock. When the dough was mixed, she took a small handful and showed the children how to wrap it around the end of a stick. The children had fun cooking

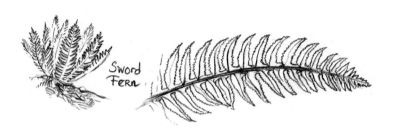
Sword Fern

the bannock over low coals, rotating their sticks to cook it evenly. When the bannock was golden brown, Ada asked everyone to hold hands. Then she faced the cedar tree and said in a powerful voice:

Licorice Fern roots make a delicious tea

*O friend,*
*Grandmother Cedar Tree, long life giver,*
*O friends,*
*the seaweeds and animals of the ocean,*
*Thank you for providing food, medicine, shelter,*
*and what we need for the circle of life.*
*O friends, long life givers.*

Then, with a twinkle in her eyes, she said, "Let the feast begin!"

The fresh bannock was heavenly with butter and jam. Crystal wondered if the nettle tea would sting her mouth. Touching stinging nettles really hurt.

Red Huckleberry

"Boiling the water takes the sting out of nettles," Ada assured her. "The nettle is good for our health, and the licorice fern roots make the tea taste delicious."

Next, Aunt Kate passed around a tray of large clamshells filled with fish soup. Uncle Charlie, Aunt Kate, and Ada loved fish soup, and they quickly devoured their portions. At first, Sam and Crystal took tiny sips of the broth, not sure they would like it, but to their surprise the soup was very pleasant. They could taste fresh Spring Salmon, halibut, potatoes, wild onions, and seaweed. Aunt Kate had also added wild Beach Peas and fresh Sea Asparagus.

Wild Strawberries grow on rock sea cliffs

On some shorelines, Wild Beach Peas grow above the Spray Zone

← each pod carries several peas

slice and dry to make kelp chips

kelp bulb dried for bottle

kelp & cream cheese donuts

Peel off outer skin for kelp donuts

kelp & cream cheese donuts

Finally, Aunt Kate passed around a tray of kelp chips and kelp slices filled with cream cheese. The kelp chips tasted a lot like potato chips, but the kelp slices took a little getting used to.

Suddenly, a handsome and mysterious black bird of the wilderness, much larger than a crow, landed on a low-hanging branch of Grandmother Cedar Tree. It seemed to be talking to itself, mixing croaks, clicks, gurgles, and bill claps in an entertaining pattern of bird rumblings: **CR-R-RUCK, CR-R-RUCK** and **TOK, TOK!**

Ada smiled. "In my culture, Raven is both a teacher and a trickster."

Crystal and Sam would have been content to listen to the bird's ramblings a while longer. But just then, their peaceful scene was interrupted by an explosive sound:

# KABOOM!

Shells of Horse Clam used as food dishes and ladles

A fresh Beach Salad

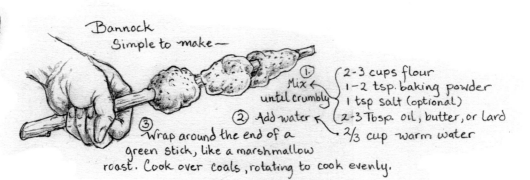

Bannock
Simple to make —

Mix until crumbly
① 2-3 cups flour
1-2 tsp. baking powder
1 tsp salt (optional)
2-3 Tbsp. oil, butter, or lard
② Add water ⅔ cup warm water
③ Wrap around the end of a green stick, like a marshmallow roast. Cook over coals, rotating to cook evenly.

# A Killer Whale Named Hope

"What was that?" yelled Sam.

"KILLER WHALES BELOW CEDAR TREE LOOKOUT!" announced Uncle Charlie, who knew the sound well.

Sam shot up from the table, followed by Crystal, Uncle Charlie, Aunt Kate, and Ada. They stood at the edge of the cliff as a pod of thirty Killer Whales passed at full speed below Cedar Tree Lookout, heading north towards Arrow Head Island.

The tall black dorsal fins of the bull orcas cut the water as the shorter, more curved fins of the females disappeared underwater and reappeared in majestic motion. One of the largest bulls swam to the surface like a torpedo and leaped clear out of the water, as if it wanted to fly. Then it fell back with an huge splash that could be seen and heard for miles.

## KABOOM!

"WAAHOO!" yelled Sam. "Awesome!"

Just when they thought it couldn't get any better, a beautiful baby Killer Whale surfaced alongside its mother.

"That calf is only two or three weeks old!" exclaimed Aunt Kate, almost in tears. "Oh, this is wonderful! It will bring new hope to the family."

"What do you mean?" asked Crystal.

"The population of Killer Whales along this coast has been falling in recent years, so every baby born is a significant event," explained Aunt Kate. "Fishermen have been taking too many salmon, and pollution is harming the environment and all the plants and animals. Because the Killer Whale is at the top of a complex food chain, it carries in its body all the toxic chemicals that are present in its prey."

"Yes," explained Ada. "These Killer Whales feed mostly on salmon, but those that travel farther out to sea also prey on seals, sea lions, porpoises, and even other whales. Toxic chemicals in the bodies of whatever a Killer Whale eats builds up in its body."

"What can we do help the Killer Whales?" asked Sam.

"I'm glad you asked that question," said Ada, and Aunt Kate nodded. "Killer Whales are in trouble because people don't ask the right questions and they don't make the right decisions."

"How will we know to make the right decisions?" asked Sam.

"The fact that you asked that question shows that you are concerned about your brothers and sisters in the animal world," said Ada. "My people say never take more salmon than you need. If you take a salmon, you should eat every part of it. The Elders say, 'If you look inside yourself, you will make the right decisions.'"

Sam and Crystal were puzzled. They didn't know what Ada meant by "look inside yourself."

As the pod of whales turned northeast towards Halibut Passage, Sam and Crystal watched in silence, wishing the newborn Killer Whale a safe journey.

"Let's name the newborn whale Hope," said Crystal. "Maybe the name will keep it safe."

**"TOK, TOK, CR-R-R-RUCK!"** croaked Raven as if in agreement.

Aunt Kate, Uncle Charlie, Ada, Crystal, and Sam spun around just in time to see Raven standing in the middle of the table. In his haste to grab a kelp slice, Raven knocked over Crystal's bowl of fish chowder, making a great big mess! Then in a flash he grabbed Uncle Charlie's stick of delicious bannock in his claws and flew with it high into the sky.

"HEY, YOU RASCAL! THAT'S MY BANNOCK!" yelled Uncle Charlie.

"You mean it *was* your bannock," joked Sam.

Then, as if showing off, Raven did a barrel roll before swooping down and disappearing into the forest.

Everyone had to laugh at Raven's antics, even Uncle Charlie.

**After they finished** their meal, Ada told the children more about Raven's intelligence and playfulness. She also told them about other animals that had special meaning to her people.

"Eagle is known for her courage and wisdom, Hummingbird for her hard work, and Killer Whale for its strength and strong family bonds. Our culture respects these animals so much that some of us belong to the clan of Eagle, some to the clan of Raven, and some to the clan of Hummingbird. I am proud to belong to the clan of Killer Whale."

Sam and Crystal had lots of questions about these clans and what they meant. They listened to Ada's stories, fascinated.

"Hey," said Sam suddenly. "Are there any stories about the creatures of the Low Tide Zone?"

"Yes, our stories, artwork, and dances involve clams, sea stars, sea urchins, octopus, and many more."

Ada was silent for a long time. Then, in a soft voice that swept across the water like a gentle breeze, she said, "Today we saw the Trickster Raven. Today the Killer Whales showed themselves. Perhaps we can think about Grandfather Sculpin, the ancient one from the sea. He is wise and could teach the children all about the animals that live in the Low Tide Zone, because they are all cousins. Perhaps he will come to take us to his world."

"Who is Grandfather Sculpin?" asked a curious Sam. "How could anyone take us through the Low Tide Zone when the tide won't be low until next week?"

"Don't worry," assured Ada. "Grandfather Sculpin knows all about life at the seashore. All the seashore creatures are his cousins and they all live together. The Elders say, 'If you teach the children to listen to the seashore, the wind, and the animals, they will teach you things.'"

Sam and Crystal had no idea what Ada was talking about. But she seemed to know something they didn't. The mystery hung in the air, and no one said anything for a few minutes.

It was Uncle Charlie who broke the silence. "Tomorrow I'm going fishing on the *Blue Heron*. Anybody want to come with me?"

"Count me in!" said Sam enthusiastically.

"Me too," added Crystal.

The two children were happy that they had seen White-sided Dolphins and Harbour Seals, Sea Otters and Bald Eagles, Tufted Puffins and Ravens, Hermit Crabs, Purple Shore Crabs, Northern Clingfish, and even Killer Whales. Tomorrow morning they would go fishing with Uncle Charlie, and perhaps Grandfather Sculpin—whoever he was—would come and take them through the Low Tide Zone, with or without a good low tide.

Sam and Crystal could hardly wait!

# Eagle Cove List of Organisms

Look for the plants and animals of Halibut Passage and Eagle Cove on
or near many rocky seashores throughout the Pacific Northwest.

## TREES, SHRUBS, FERNS
Beach Peas
Douglas Fir
Licorice Fern
Oregon Grape
Red Huckleberry
Salal
Sea Asparagus
Shore Pine
Sitka Spruce
Stinging Nettle
Sword Fern
Western Red Cedar
Wild Strawberries

## BIRDS
**(warm blooded, egg laying)**
Bald Eagle
Common Murre
Glaucous-winged Gull
Raven
Tufted Puffin

## MAMMALS (warm blooded, nourish young with milk)
California Sea Lion
Harbour Seal
Killer Whale
Mink
Pacific White-sided Dolphin
Sea Otter

## FISHES
**(cold blooded, gills and fins)**
High Cockscomb Blenny
Northern Clingfish
Tidepool Sculpin

## ARTHROPODS (jointed legs)
Coon-striped Shrimp
Decorator Crab
Gooseneck Barnacle
Hairy Hermit Crab
Kelp Flea
Purple Shore Crab
Red Rock Crab
Rock Louse
Small Acorn Barnacle

## ECHINODERNS (spiny skins)
Purple or Orange Sea Star
Red Sea Urchin
Sunflower Sea Star

## MOLLUSKS (muscular foot)
Black Chiton
California Blue Mussel
Checkered Periwinkle
Keyhole Limpet
Lined Chiton
Pacific Octopus
Sitka Periwinkle
Speckled Limpet
Wrinkled Whelk

## CNIDARIA (stinging cells)
Giant Green Sea Anemone
Pink-tipped Sea Anemone

## SEAWEEDS
Bull Kelp
Giant Kelp
Perennial Kelp
Rockweed
Sea Lettuce
Sea Sac
Surf Grass